Shark!

by

Michaela Morgan

Illustrated by Shona Grant

First published in 2006 in Great Britain by
Barrington Stoke Ltd
18 Walker St, Edinburgh, EH3 7LP

www.barringtonstoke.co.uk

Reprinted 2007

ISBN: 978-1-84299-439-9

Printed in Great Britain by Bell & Bain Ltd

A Note from the Author

OK, I admit it. I'm a wimp.

I live near the sea but I don't like to go into it.

I don't like water going in my eyes.

I don't like sea-weed.

I'm scared of jelly-fish. And there might be sharks!

Everyone tells me not to be a fool. "There aren't any sharks here!" they all say.

But I'm not happy.

You never know …

For Ben, Matthew and Jamie

Contents

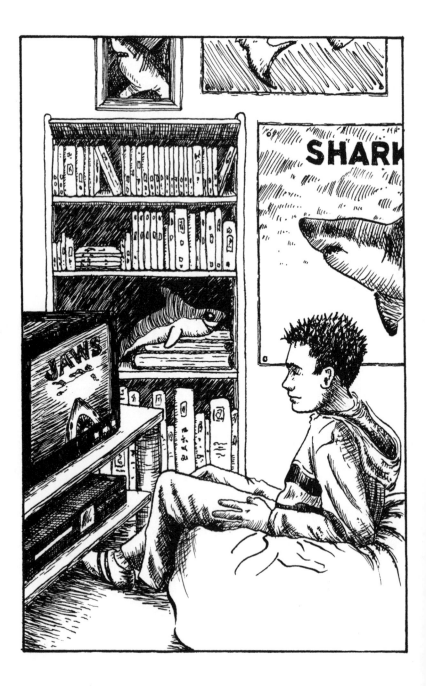

Chapter 1
Sharky Mark

Mark was mad about sharks. That's why his brother called him Sharky Mark.

Mark had seen the film *Jaws* when he was six.

Then he'd seen it again.

And again.

And again.

He was 15 years old now and he had lost count of how many times he had seen it.

He had books about sharks.

He had posters of sharks,

and photos of sharks.

He had DVDs and videos of sharks.

When he was little he even had a cuddly toy shark.

It was still in his room – a little bit dusty and sad-looking now, but there it still was.

"He's mad about sharks," his mum said.

"He's just mad," said Connor, his big brother.

But Mark wanted *more* than shark stories and cartoons and films.

He wanted facts. Hard facts. He started to keep a record of every shark story, every news report, every bit of shark information that he could find.

He kept a Shark File. As the years went by, Mark's scrapbook of shark stories grew and grew.

It was full of pages like this:

Hammerhead Shark
10-footer   Hunting

Great White
with diver

Seal hunting

Mark became a real shark expert.

"Maybe you can work with sharks when you leave school," his mum said.

"No chance," said his brother, Connor. "You'll never even get to *see* a real shark!"

"Well ..." said Mum. "Have I got news for you!"

Chapter 2
Good News

The news was good! It was better than good. It was *great!*

Mum had really got her act together. She had got them tickets to fly to Florida for their holidays!

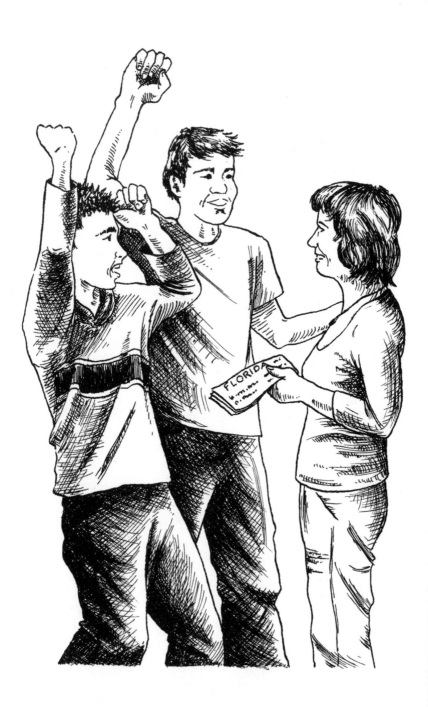

"Florida, USA?" asked Connor.

"The *real* Florida – in America?" asked Mark.

It seemed too good to be true.

"You always say we're broke!" Mark pointed out.

"Well ..." Mum said, "I got a really great deal on the tickets. The price was right! But better – even better ... your Uncle Alan has got a flat in Florida – right near a beach. We can stay there – for free. So it's sorted!"

"We can go to Disney World!" said Connor.

"And Shark World!" Mum grinned at Mark.

"Better yet!" said Mark. "We can see real sharks in the sea!"

"In your dreams," said Connor.

Mark did spend the next weeks
dreaming of his holiday. So did Connor.

They had to find the right clothes.

The right bag.

And Mark had to find out all about
sharks in Florida.

"You're not taking that scrap book with
you, are you!" Connor mocked.

"It's my Fact File," said Mark. "Packed with info that might be very handy."

"Such as?"

"Such as this," said Mark and he opened Page 13 ...

TIPS TO AVOID SHARK ATTACKS

1) Always stay in groups not too far from the shore.

2) Never carry dead fish when swimming
    and diving.

3) Don't swim at night or early morning.
    These are the shark's hunting times.

4) Stay out of dirty or cloudy water.

5) Never swim close to sharks.

6) Do not enter the water if you are
    bleeding.

7) Do not wear anything shiny, e.g. chains or rings. This looks like fish scales to a shark.

Connor fell about laughing. "Right!" he said.

"I will make sure I don't go paddling in dirty water. All alone. Wearing bling. And bleeding. I won't go first thing in the morning or in the middle of the night. And I will never, *never* carry a dead fish. Then I should be OK!"

Connor went off still laughing. Mark could hear him singing:

"My brother is a lame brain

My brother is a lame brain

What a dork!

What a dork!"

"I don't care," Mark muttered and he packed his Fact File into his bag.

But all that week he had to put up with Connor's jokes.

"Did you know that a shark will only attack you if you're wet?

My brother, Mark is a big drip so he'd better watch out!"

Chapter 3
Shark Heaven

At last the big day came. Their holiday
began.

They had an early start. A *very* early
start!

Then they had a long flight – a *very* long flight. But in the end they got to Florida.

Mum rented a car to drive them to the motel. They were going to stay in a motel in town for a week. Then they were going to drive to Uncle Alan's place near the sea.

The week went by in a blur of sunshine and days out. They went all over the place.

Disney World was great.

Water World was wicked.

But best of all – for Mark – was Shark World.

He was in Shark Heaven. He, Connor and their mum went through a tunnel. Sharks swam over them. Sharks swam under them. Sharks swam all around them. Their black bodies swam by, swift and silent. Their teeth shone sharp and white. Their glassy eyes stared at Mark. And Mark stared back.

He knew something about each shark. He could spot them all and he had all the facts.

"That's a Basking Shark," he said, "and wow, look, that's a Great White!"

One of the men working by the shark tank looked at Mark. "You seem to know your sharks," he said.

"Yes, I do!" said Mark.

"He does ..." Connor groaned. "He drives us crazy with his sharks. He's been mad about them ever since he started to talk, and he never stops talking about them. We call him Sharky Mark."

Mark looked at the Shark World man, standing there in his Shark World T-shirt, keeping an eye on the sharks. "Do you work here? All the time?"

The man nodded. "I got my first job here helping out when I was only a bit older than you."

"You're really lucky," said Mark. "Do you think *I* could get a job like you with sharks?"

"It's possible!" the man replied. "There are Shark Parks all over the world. Ask for an Information Pack at the desk by the exit. It tells you all about working with sharks. There's even an Application Form."

Mark didn't need telling twice. Quicker than you can say *Hammerhead shark* he was at the Information Desk, and he read the Information Pack as soon as he got back to the motel. There was a list of all the

Shark Worlds in the world. There was one in England.

The Application Form asked all the normal stuff:

Name

Address

School

But the last page asked:

What experience have you had with sharks?

There was a big blank page to fill in.

Mark sighed. He hadn't had *any* experience with sharks. How do you get experience with sharks when you live in Leeds? There would be nothing in his Application Form that would make him stand out from all the other kids who would like to work at a Shark World. It was hopeless.

Chapter 4
The Sea

At the end of the first week of their holiday, Mark, Connor and their mum packed all their stuff in a hired car and drove off to the sea.

"Look at the sea!" Mum cried. "Look at the trees ... the birds! Fantastic!"

But Mark and Connor didn't care about trees and birds. All Connor could think about was girls in bikinis. All Mark could think about was getting close to the sea. He wanted to see sharks swimming in the open sea. He peered out of the car window and tried to spot one.

"There aren't any sharks here, lame brain," said his big brother. "Do you think anyone would come on holiday and swim in a sea full of sharks!"

"You're the lame brain," Mark snapped. "There are loads of sharks on this coast. Loads of shark attacks too!"

"That can't be true," said Mum. "We'll ask your Uncle Alan when we arrive."

And that's what they did. They sat outside Alan's house chatting as they watched the sun set.

"It's true," Alan said. "There are sharks. But there's no danger. Sharks stay out at sea. There have been attacks – but not often!" He smiled at Mark. "You're much more likely to be attacked by a jellyfish!"

"But much less likely to be *eaten* by a jellyfish," said Mark.

"True!" Alan grinned. "But, you know, sharks don't like to eat people. They don't like the taste!"

"Ha! You see," said Connor.

"I know, I know ..." said Mark. "Sharks don't *like* to eat human flesh. They don't like it – but that won't stop them biting! A person in the sea can look like a seal – or a big fish – to a shark. The shark takes a bite of you just to see if you taste nice. Then he might spit you out. *But* by then you will have bled to death – or drowned."

"Give it a rest," Connor groaned. "We're all going fishing with Alan tomorrow. You'll put us off."

"I'm not going," said Mum. "Too early in the morning for me."

"I'll go," said Mark. "I'll take my new camera. Might get a snap of a shark! Boy snaps shark! Get it?"

They all laughed.

Chapter 5

Fishing

It was still dark next morning when Mark was woken up. "Time to go," said Connor. "The early fisherman catches the fish. Gotta be early if you wanna catch fish!"

"I've put everything we need in the car," said Uncle Alan. "I've put in a surf board, three rods, nets, and two buckets of bait!"

Connor held his nose when he smelt the fish in the bait bucket. He peered in. Small dead fish, fish heads, fish guts. It smelt of fish and blood and sea-weed.

"Disgusting!" he said.

"See you later." Mum waved. "Take plenty of pictures to show me."

Uncle Alan had given Mark a digital camera. He'd given Connor a diver's watch.

The sun was just rising when they arrived at the beach. Alan and Connor went off to fish. Alan stood on a rock by the sea and Connor waded in. Mark sat on a rock, with his shark notebook and camera. He watched the sun beginning to grow and glow. Slowly, slowly the day was coming to life.

He laid the small surf board – what Uncle Alan called the boogie board – by his side. Maybe he'd have a go later, but for the moment he just wanted to watch the sea and the sun. He peered out to sea and flicked through his Shark File. He got to:

TIPS TO AVOID SHARK ATTACKS

1) Always stay in groups not too far from the shore.

2) Never carry dead fish when swimming and diving.

3) Don't swim at night or early morning. These are the shark's hunting times.

4) Stay out of dirty or cloudy water.

5) Never swim close to a shark.

6) Do not enter the water if you are bleeding.

7) Do not wear anything shiny e.g. chains or rings. This looks like fish scales to a shark.

Mark skimmed through the list and then he read again –

7) Do not wear anything shiny e.g. chains or rings. This looks like fish scales to a shark.

Wasn't Connor wearing his new diver's watch? And a chain round his neck? Mark looked out to sea. He could see Connor standing deep in the water. He waved and shouted, "Hey, Connor!" Connor waved back. And as he waved, the sun glinted off his watch.   .

Mark's heart seemed to stop. He felt cold. He went through the list in his head.

Connor was wearing his shiny new diver's watch.

He was standing *alone* in the sea.

It was early in the morning.

And with him he had a bucket of bait. Bait that was made of bits of fish, fish heads, fish guts, blood and – dead fish.

Connor would make the perfect target for a shark.

Chapter 6
Shark

A chill ran down Mark's back. He knew, he just knew something was going to happen. He could feel it.

He looked out to sea and peered and peered. Nothing.

"It's too far away to see anything," Mark thought. Then he had an idea. He looked through the camera and used the zoom lens. Now he could see everything much bigger.

He looked from left to right, he looked far out to sea. Way out at sea he saw a line of rippling water. Could it be? No, it couldn't! Surely it couldn't? He stared and stared – was that the tip of a fin? Was that a sharp black fin tip slicing like a knife towards his brother?

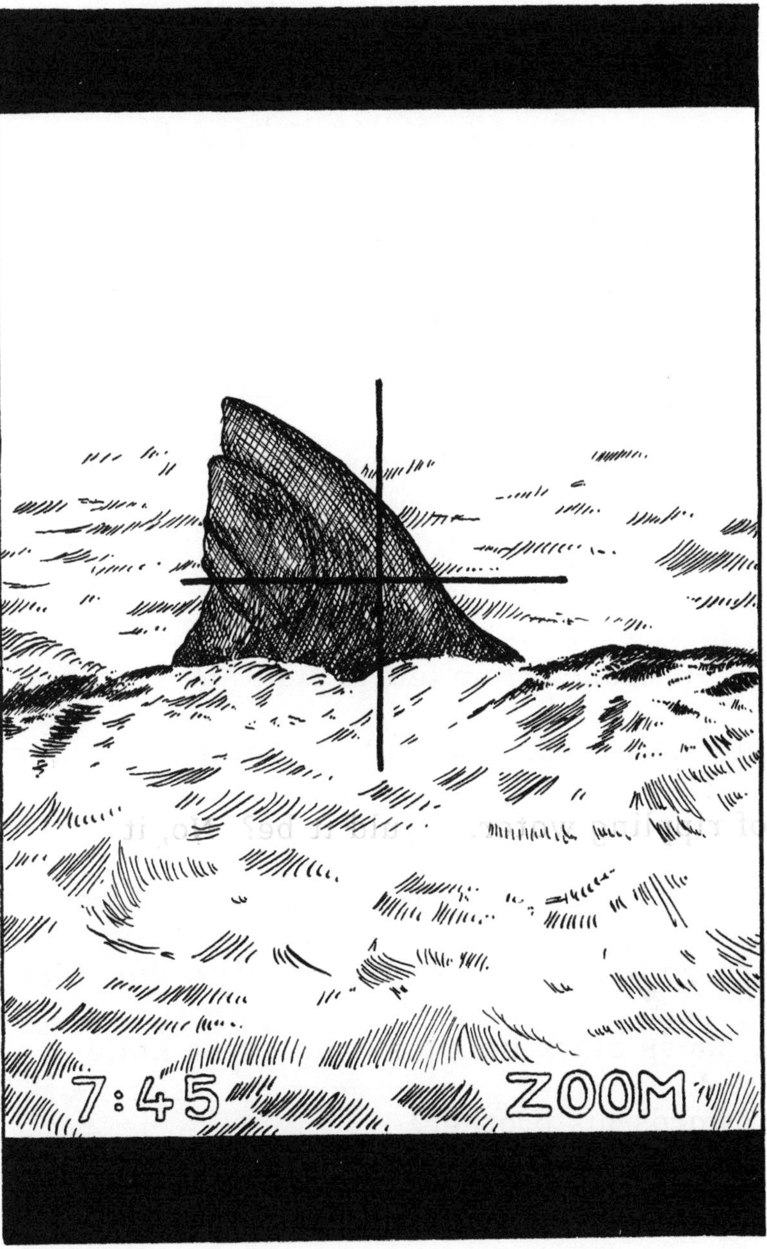
7:45
ZOOM

Mark leapt to his feet and ran towards the sea, shouting, "Connor! *Connor!* Get out of the sea. Get out!"

Maybe Connor didn't hear.

Maybe he didn't care.

He stayed still, standing where he was, waist deep in water with the bucket of bait over his arm. The ripples in the water were closer to him now. They were going round and round him in a large circle. The shark was circling him!

Then Connor saw the fin. "Oh my G ..." he started, but before he could finish he saw Mark running towards him through the water.

Mark was carrying the surf board under his left arm and with his right arm he was grabbing for the bucket of bait.

"What ..." Connor began and then the shark's nose reared out of the water.

They could smell its fishy breath.

They could look into its hard glassy eyes.

They could see its razor teeth.

Mark swung the bucket of bait and hit out hard at the shark's snout. Then he flung the bait bucket and the surf board out as far as he could. He heard a snap and a ripping but felt no pain.

But a stream of blood ran from his arm into the sea.

Chapter 7
Police

Mark and Connor held on to each other and made for the shore. Any moment they expected to hear the snap of the shark's jaws closing in on them, but they made it back to the beach.

Alan, who had heard the shouting, was there to help them. "What is it? What ..." he cried.

The two boys fell onto the beach. They were shaking, feeling weak. It was then that Alan saw Mark's arm. Blood was pouring from it. He tied his shirt tightly around the bleeding arm and pushed the boys into the car.

"Hospital!" he said. "There's one near here. Hang on!"

He drove like the wind.

It wasn't long before the police saw them speeding and stopped them. A police officer walked towards their car. He opened his book but Connor yelled at him.

"We've got to get to a hospital! My brother's been bitten by a shark."

"Follow me!" said the policeman. They drove behind the police car with its lights flashing, its siren blaring, and screeched to a stop at the hospital.

Chapter 8
Big News

It didn't take long for the newspaper people to arrive. And the TV crews. Everyone was going crazy.

Connor and Mark stood in front of the cameras and told their story. Mark's arm was in a sling.

"It's not a deep bite," Mark said. "The shark's jaws closed around the bait bucket and didn't sink too deeply in my arm. It should be OK in two or three weeks. I've got a bad cut. And some ripped tendons. And I'll have a scar."

Mark felt proud of his scar. A shark bite scar!

"And," he said, "I've got this ..." He held out his hand and showed a shark tooth. "This tooth was left in my arm."

He told the reporters how he had spotted the shark and how he had run to save his brother.

"I knew what to do," he boasted to the reporters. "I know a lot about sharks. I threw the boogie board out to sea. To a shark, the shape of a boogie board looks like a seal. So the shark turned to chase that. Then I threw the bucket of bait. Blood and fish guts attract sharks. So, while the shark was going after that, we were able to escape."

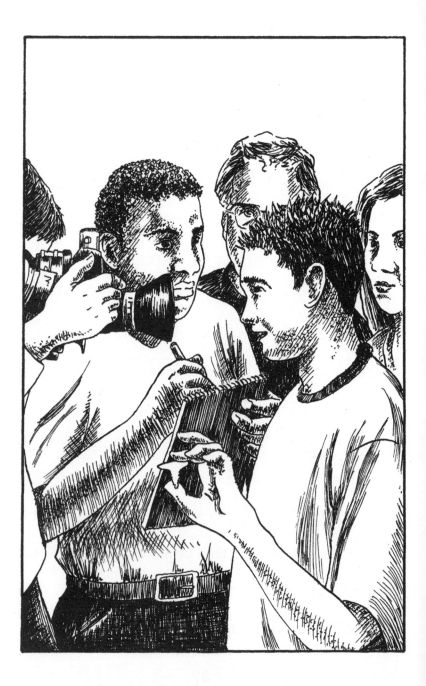

Mark's story was in all the newspapers and it was on TV too. When Mark came back home to England it was big news there too. Mark proudly cut out every report and added them to his Shark File. He put the tooth on a chain and wore it round his neck, and he smiled to himself because he knew what he was going to do.

When it was time to look for a job he was going to apply to work in a Shark Park. And when it got to the page where it asked: "What experience have you had with sharks?" he had a story to tell that was going to get him the job, and the life, of his dreams.

Barrington Stoke would like to thank all its readers for commenting on the manuscript before publication and in particular:

Amber Anderson

Jordan Baillie

Naomi Bell

Lana Benson

Eve Campbell

Kerr Gibson

Helen Hale

Nicole Harland

Sarah Marshall

Robert Mitchell

S. Peet

Kirsty Raeburn

Jordan Shaw

Evelyn Smith

Elan Tang

Sam Thake

Stephanie Tumulka

Sarah Willis

Elizabeth Wilson

Become a Consultant!

Would you like to give us feedback on our titles before they are published? Contact us at the address below – we'd love to hear from you!

Email: info@barringtonstoke.co.uk
Website: www.barringtonstoke.co.uk

Also by the same author ...

Respect!

by

Michaela Morgan

When their mum and dad die, Tully and his little brother only have each other.

They are sent to a Children's Home.

The other kids make fun of them.

But Tully has an amazing talent which will win him a place in history.

gr8reads

You can order *Respect!* directly from our website at **www.barringtonstoke.co.uk**

More exciting NEW titles ...

Speed
by
Alison Prince

The Need for Speed

Deb loves to drive fast.

The faster, the better.

Until she goes too far, too fast ...

You can order *Speed* directly from our website at
www.barringtonstoke.co.uk

More exciting NEW titles ...

Fight
by
Chris Powling

My Mate Could Take You ...

Matt's mate is a big, tough guy.

So that must make Matt hard too ...

Or does it?

gr8reads

You can order *Fight* directly from our website at
www.barringtonstoke.co.uk